Max and Zoe

at School

by Shelley Swanson Sateren

illustrated by Mary Sullivan

PICTURE WINDOW BOOKS

a capstone imprint

Max and Zoe is published by Picture Window Books
a Capstone Imprint
1710 Roe Crest Drive
North Mankato, Minnesota 56003
www.capstonepub.com

Copyright © 2012 by Picture Window Books

Library of Congress Cataloging-in-Publication Data
Sateren, Shelley Swanson.
Max and Zoe at school / by Shelley Swanson Sateren ; illustrated by Mary Sullivan.
p. cm. -- (Max and Zoe)
Summary: Max learns the importance of keeping his desk clean, with help from his friend Zoe.
ISBN 978-1-4048-6211-1 (library binding)
[1. Orderliness--Fiction. 2. Desks--Fiction. 3. Schools--Fiction.
4. Friendship--Fiction.] I. Sullivan, Mary, 1958- ill. II. Title.
PZ7.S249155Map 2011
[E]--dc22

2011006497

Art Director: Kay Fraser
Designer: Emily Harris

Printed in China.
0312/CA21200232
012012   006583R

Table of Contents

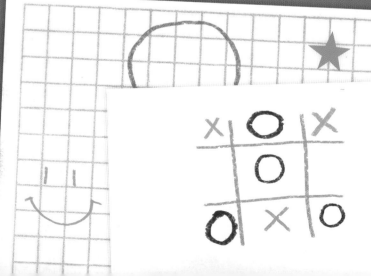

Max and Zoe sat next to each other in school.

One Friday afternoon, Max's pencil rolled off his desk.

"Not again," he said.

"Hey," Zoe whispered.
"I've picked this up five times today!"

"Sorry," Max said.

"No talking, please," said Ms. Young.

"Sorry," said Zoe. "But Max's pencil keeps rolling off his desk. His desk won't close."

Ms. Young looked at Max's desk.

"Oh, my! I think it's
time to clean our desks,"
Ms. Young said.

Max raised his desktop.
Papers and trash flew out.
Crayons, books, and toys fell
out, too.

"I can't clean this!" Max
said. "It's too messy!"

He tried to close it again.

But too much junk stuck out.

"Oh, dear. I'm afraid
you'll have to stay inside
and clean," Ms. Young said.

"But it's snowing," Zoe

whispered to Max.

"I know," he said. "I want

to build a snow fort!"

"Me, too. I'll help you

clean. Get going!" Zoe said.

Max tried to clean. But

he couldn't stop watching

the snow. Max had to miss

recess.

Chapter 2
A Month of Homework

"Thanks for staying inside

to help me, Zoe," Max said.

"You're welcome. But stop

looking at the snow. We'll

make a fort after school,"

she said.

"Okay." Max frowned at his desk. "I don't even know where to start."

"Take everything out. Put it all on the floor," said Zoe.

"Gross! A rotten apple," Max said.

"Focus, Max. Make three piles," said Zoe. "Trash. School. Home."

They began to sort. They worked fast.

Max saw some papers in
a folder. "Uh-oh," he said.

"Your family tree
homework!" Zoe said. "You
haven't even started it!"

"I guess I left it in my desk," Max said.

"You were supposed to work on that all month. It's due on Monday!" Zoe said.

"Oops. I'm in trouble," Max said.

After school, Max pulled

on his snow pants. He and

Zoe were going to build a

giant snow fort!

"Max, take off your snow

gear," said Mom.

"What! Why?" Max

asked.

She held up the folder.

"We've got a lot of work

to do. Let's get started," she

said.

Chapter 3
The Note

Monday morning, Max and Zoe sat together on the school bus.

"Don't lose that folder again," said Zoe.

"I won't. No more desk dump for me!" Max said.

At school, Max opened

his desk. "What's this?"

A big sheet of folded

paper was stuffed inside.

Max took it to Ms. Young.

"Somebody messed up

my desk," he said.

"Open it, and read it to

the class," Ms. Young said.

The note was from

Ms. Young!

Excellent Job!

You have the cleanest desk in our room!

At recess, I'll come outside with our class. We can stay out an extra 10 minutes!

Have fun!

Everyone clapped.

"Way to go, Max!" Zoe said.

And at recess, Max and Zoe finally got to make a super cool fort.

About the Author

Shelley Swanson Sateren is the author of many children's books and has worked as an editor and a bookseller. Today, besides writing, she works with children aged five to twelve in an after-school program. At home or at the cabin, Shelley loves to read, watch movies, cross-country ski, and walk. She lives in St. Paul, Minnesota, with her husband and two sons.

About the Illustrator

Mary Sullivan has been drawing and writing her whole life, which has mostly been spent in Texas. She earned her BFA from the University of Texas in Studio Art, but she considers herself a self-trained illustrator. Mary lives in Cedar Park, a suburb of Austin, Texas.

Glossary

focus (FOH-kuhss) — to concentrate on something or somebody

fort (FORT) — a place to gather and hang out; similar to a clubhouse

homework (HOME-wurk) — work you get at school that you have to do at home

recess (REE-sess) — a break from work for fun or relaxation

rotten (ROT-uhn) — bad

sort (SORT) — to separate things into groups

Discussion Questions

1. Zoe helped Max clean out his desk. Talk about a time when you helped a friend.

2. Why is it important to do your homework on time?

3. After Max cleaned his desk, the class got an extra ten minutes at recess. Do you think this was a good reward? Why or why not?

Writing Prompts

1. Max and Zoe like to build snow forts. Make a list of three things you like to do in the snow.

2. Max finds a rotten apple when he cleans his desk. What's the strangest thing you've found when cleaning? Write a sentence about it.

3. What was your favorite part of this story? Write a few sentences about it.

Make Your Own Fort

In the story, Max and Zoe built a snow fort outside. You can build a great fort inside your home, too.

What you need:
- sheets
- blankets
- pillows
- sofa cushions
- cardboard boxes
- a flashlight
- toys

What you do:

1. Clear an area around a sofa or bed.

2. Prop sofa cushions near the sofa or bed to form the walls of the fort. Use chairs, if necessary, to prop up the cushions.

3. Build the roof by draping sheets over the cushions.

4. Create a door with another sheet or blanket. Or build a tunnel entrance by tilting cushions together.

5. Use cushions, blankets, and cardboard boxes to make furniture for your fort.

6. Add toys and other items to decorate your fort. Use flashlights for lights.

The Fun Doesn't Stop Here!

Discover more at www.capstonekids.com

- Videos & Contests
- Games & Puzzles
- Friends & Favorites
- Authors & Illustrators

Find cool websites and more books like this one at www.facthound.com. Just type in the Book ID **9781404862111** and you're ready to go!